Grandma's Christmas Wish

To Jean Ferris and her grandson, EJ.
—Helen Foster James

*

For Ivy

— Petra Brown

Sleeping Bear Press™

2395 South Huron Parkway, Suite 200
Ann Arbor, MI 48104
www.sleepingbearpress.com

Printed and bound in the United States.

10 9 8 7 6 5 4 3 2 1

Library of Congress Cataloging-in-Publication Data

James, Helen Foster, 1951-
Grandma's Christmas wish / by Helen Foster James ;
illustrated by Petra Brown.
pages cm
Summary: A rabbit grandmother celebrates the
infant who is her best Christmas gift of all.
ISBN 978-1-58536-918-8
[1. Stories in rhyme. 2. Grandmothers–Fiction. 3. Babies–Fiction. 4.
Christmas–Fiction.] I. Brown, Petra, illustrator. II. Title.
PZ8.3.J1477Gt 2015
[E]–dc23
2015001568

This book is presented to:

_____

On this day:

_____

Grandma's

Christmas Wish

Written by Helen Foster James

Illustrated by Petra Brown

Your grandma loves you.
I love you, I do.

Jingle bells baby.
Adorable you.

My wish for Christmas
is certain to be

some kisses and hugs
from you . . . just for me.

We'll have our stockings
and under the tree,

there will be presents
for you and for me.

GRAN

But, you with your grin
and all of your charms,

you're my best present,
just wrapped in my arms.

You fill up my heart
with holiday cheer.

I love you, my love,
my snowflake, my dear.

You're like the star on
the first Christmas night,

a sparkle of joy,
a twinkle of light.

A candy cane kiss
I have just for you.

Giggles and cuddles
and mistletoe, too.

You're a "grand" baby,
an angel, it's true,

and no gift could be
as precious as you!

A Special Letter to My Grandchild

_____

_____

_____

_____

_____

_____

_____

With Love, _____

Paste a picture of grandma
and grandchild here.

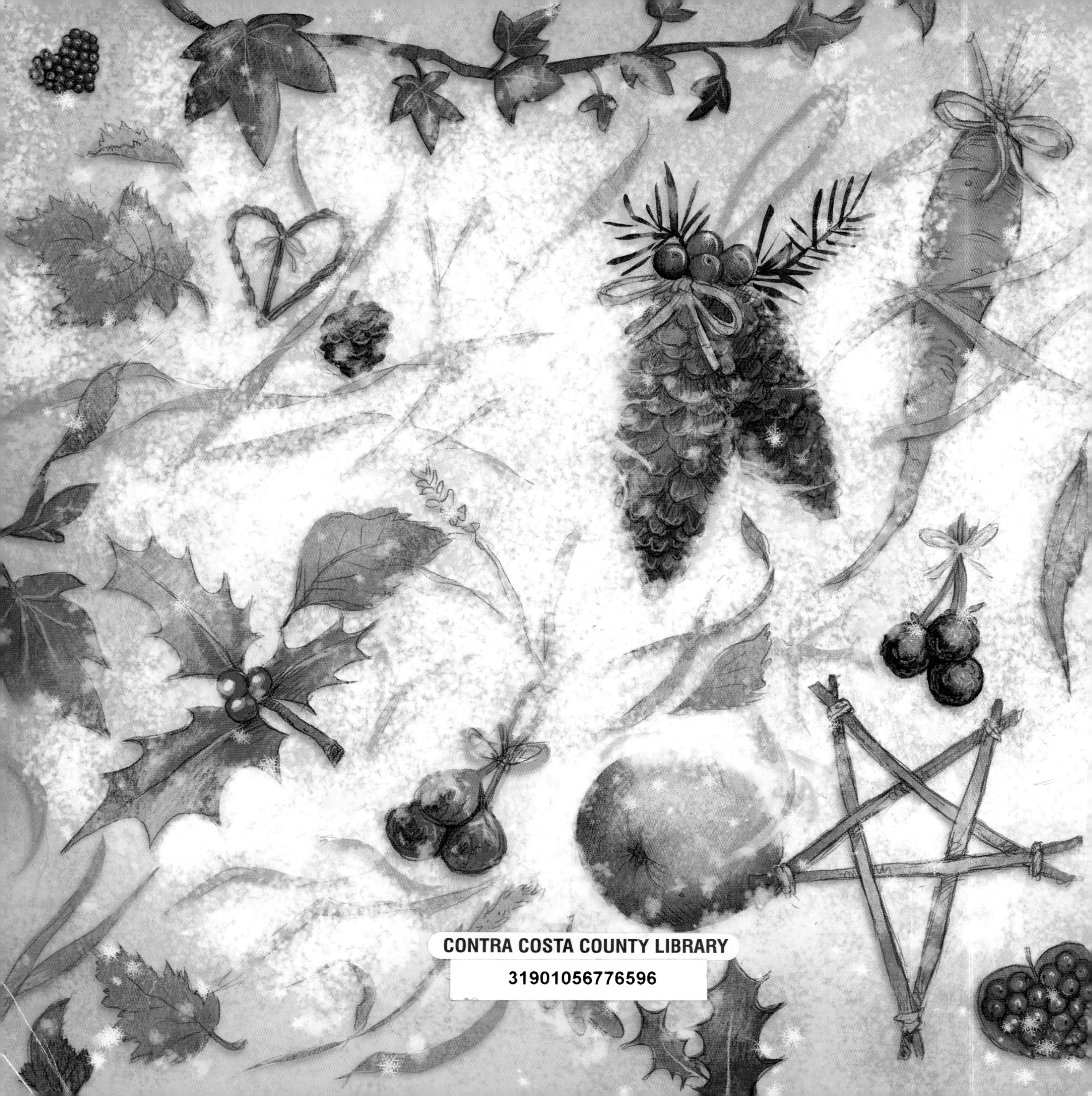